Meet the Care Bears

by
Ali Reich

illustrated by
J. M. L. Gray

A Care Bear™ Book from Random House, New York

Copyright © 1983 by American Greetings Corporation. Care Bears and Care Bear are trademarks of American Greetings Corporation. All rights reserved under International and Pan-American Copyright Conventions. Published in the United States by Random House, Inc., New York, and simultaneously in Canada by Random House of Canada Limited, Toronto. Library of Congress Catalog Card Number: 82-61672 ISBN: 0-394-85844-1 Manufactured in the United States of America

Somewhere there's a special spot
where Care Bears live called Care-a-lot.
There Care Bears drift on clouds of fluff,
and the sun is shining just enough,

and rainbows are the slippery slides
on which the Care Bears go for rides!

In Care-a-lot they snooze and play,
but when you need them, they'll be on their way!
They'll help you do *anything* you want to do.
What Care Bears care about most is YOU!

Tenderheart Bear is a lovable guy.
He'll help you give hugs when you're feeling shy.
He's happy to play and he's happy to rest.
He's happy to do all the things you like best!

Cheer Bear is ready to brighten your day
when nothing quite seems to be going your way.
If your feelings are hurt,
   if you're sick,
      if you're sad,
Cheer Bear arrives! Things aren't so bad!

Birthday Bear's ready to wave a balloon
or sing "Happy Birthday," his favorite tune.
He goes with you to parties. He helps you have fun.
He adds magic to birthdays for *everyone*!

Wish Bear's always where you are
when you wish upon a star,
helping every wish come true,
dreaming every dream with *you*!

Grumpy Bear knows that a kid can get mad
and feel angry enough to scream and be bad!
When you pout or kick or start to cry,
Grumpy Bear will be there . . . he understands why.

Good Luck Bear has been around
where four-leaf clovers can be found.
He'll help you have a lucky day.
He'll help you win the games you play!

Funshine Bear always wears a smile.
Being happy is her style!
She helps you see the sun shine through
when things aren't going right for you!

Love-a-Lot Bear likes Valentine's Day
because it is her special way
to say "I love you"
            or
"Will you be mine?"
She wants to be *your* valentine.

Friend Bear is one Bear you can't be without.
You'll never be lonely when Friend Bear's about.
She's ready to play or to listen to you.
She's ready to go everyplace that you do!

Bedtime Bear hums you lullabies.
Just cuddle in bed and close your eyes.
Don't worry or wiggle or try counting sheep.
He brings you good dreams when you go to sleep.

When you're feeling grouchy,
when you're feeling blue,
when you're feeling lonely—
all kids sometimes do—

when happy's exactly just what you are NOT,
don't forget your Care Bear friends
in a land called Care-a-lot!